First published 2019 by Nosy Crow Ltd
The Crow's Nest, 14 Baden Place, Crosby Row, London SE1 1YW
www.nosycrow.com

ISBN 978 1 78800 875 4

Printed in Italy
Papers used by Nosy Crow are made from wood grown in sustainable forests.
1 3 5 7 9 8 6 4 2

Excitable Edgar

Written by Lucy Feather

Illustrated by Jo Lindley

nosy Crow

JOHN LEWIS
& PARTNERS

WAITROSE
& PARTNERS

*O*nce upon a wintertime –
that's where this Christmas story starts –

Ava had a dragon friend –
they couldn't bear to be apart.

Edgar was, well . . . dragonish.
Just look at him,
    it's plain to see . . .

and if a dragon gets excited,
then his breath turns . . .

fiery!

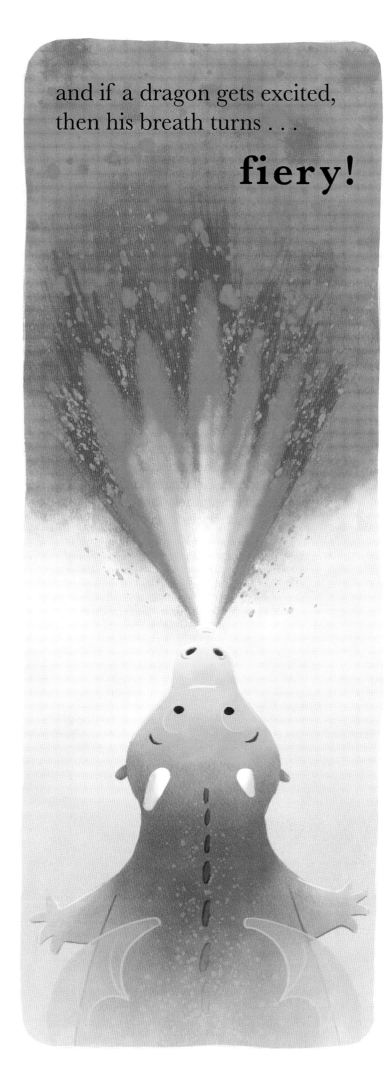

Now, hot and cold are opposites –
I'm sure that's something that you know –
so Edgar's fiery dragon breath
did **not** mix well with ice and snow.

The children built a snowman
and they laughed and cheered, delighted . . .

. . . but – oh, dear!

Snowmen turn to puddles
when a dragon gets excited.

The next day, Edgar was so careful . . .
until something caught his eye —
lots of village children skating
on the frozen pond nearby!

But can you guess what happened next?

Yes, I think that I know too . . .

Edgar's giggles melted all the ice . . .

and left them quite
wet through!

"I know it's just
that you're excited,"
Ava said and stroked his head.
"Let's keep away from
ice and snow and see
the Christmas tree instead."

The next day, they joined everyone,
all gathered in the village square,
and gazed in wonder at the Christmas
wreaths and mistletoe hung there.

Ava patted Edgar's head.
"Remember," she said, looking down.
"Keep calm! No fire! No flames! No sparks!"
He nodded with an earnest frown.

Suddenly, the drum roll started.
The crowd all counted 1, 2, 3 . . .

and there it was at last!
Hooray!
A huge and splendid
Christmas tree.

But . . . Edgar **was** a dragon,
and a dragon's not to blame
if he shakes and trembles,

and then . . .

...**WHOOSH!**
The tree goes up in flames!

The villagers all gasped in shock
as Edgar gulped and ran back home . . .

. . . he slipped into his little dragon
hut where he could cry alone.

Ava followed, knocking on
his door but there was no reply,
even though she thought she heard
the tiniest of dragon sighs.

Now, happily, I'm glad to say,
that's not where this story ends –
at this story's start I told you
that these two were best of friends.

Well, Ava couldn't bear to think
of Edgar all alone and sad.
She tried to coax him with mince pies
and told him not to feel so bad.

Ava sat and waited as
the cold day turned to snowy night . . .

. . . but Edgar just felt too embarrassed,
and he kept his door shut tight.

When best friends aren't together,
it's as if a heart is split in two . . .

Ava thought and thought and thought
and suddenly knew what to do!

While the scents of Christmas filled
the bakery, surrounding her,
Ava seized a mixing bowl
and eagerly began to stir.

When Ava woke
on Christmas Day,
she wrapped her gift,
tied ribbons too,

and as she ran to see her friend
she called . . .

"I've just the thing for you!"

Now, dragons will be dragons,
breathing fire is simply what they do . . .

. . . and when the time for pudding came,
well . . . Edgar's fire was right on cue!

So if you ever meet a dragon
who can be a little roary,
remember that a dragon's breath
can sometimes save a Christmas story . . .

Remember to spread peace and joy.
Remember that it's good to share.
Remember everyone you love.
This Christmas, show how much you care.